BirdSpell

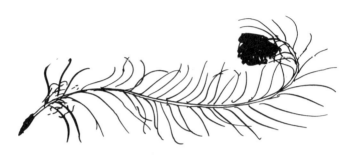

First published in Great Britain 1995
by William Heinemann Ltd
an imprint of Reed Consumer Books Limited
Michelin House, 81 Fulham Road, London SW3 6RB
and Auckland, Melbourne, Singapore and Toronto

Reprinted June 1995

ISBN 0 434 966916

A CIP catalogue record for this book is
available at the British Library

Printed in Great Britain by
Bookcraft (Bath) Ltd.

Helen Cresswell

Bird Spell

ILLUSTRATED BY AAFKE BROUWER

HEINEMANN YOUNG BOOKS

ONE

Tom didn't want to go. He had never liked fairs, though he knew you were supposed to. You were meant to like having your stomach churned and being turned inside out. You were meant to like being afraid that you might actually get killed.

'There's a new ride, Mick says – the Dice with Death. Fantabulous, he says!'

That settled it.

'Haven't got any money,' Tom said.

'Ask your mum.'

'Already had next week's pocket money.'

'I'll tell you what, I'll lend you some. I've still got all my birthday money.'

Tom was trapped. There was no way he could tell Jake the real reason why he didn't want to go to the Goose Fair. He had to think quickly. If once you got the tag of 'sissy' in Station Street, you'd got it for ever.

'Got to go to the square,' Tom said. 'Collecting car numbers.'

'Car numbers? You're joking!'

Tom himself thought that collecting car numbers was wimpish, but the words had just come out. He wished he'd thought of a better alibi.

'It's for a project,' he lied.

'Oh.'

That settled it. You couldn't argue with a project. Tom walked with Jake as far as the stop for the number twenty-three bus.

'There's an even *bigger* Big Wheel this year, Mick says.'

Tom's stomach pitched and somersaulted at the mere thought of it. If anything, he hated the Big Wheel even more than the Rotor. Each time he'd been stuck on it had seemed an eternity. He'd have given a year's pocket money to be let off it. The trouble was, once you were on, you could scream and yell all you liked, they wouldn't stop it.

The more you screamed, the more they thought you were enjoying it. He sometimes had nightmares about it.

'Fantastic,' he lied. Just then the bus drew up.

'Bring you some candy floss!' Jake told him, and was gone.

So here he was, hanging about in the square, frozen and bored stiff. He thought he'd better collect some car numbers. It would make his fib less of a fib.

He had filled two pages of his notebook when a thought struck him. 'I can just invent numbers. I'll go home and make some up. Who's to know?'

He set off, head bent against the wind. He realised he was walking between the cracks of the slabs, just like a girl. (Or like himself, not so long ago.) Deliberately he began to walk *on* the cracks, just to show that he knew it didn't matter. He half wished a bear would turn up, all growl and teeth. It would liven things up. That was when he walked into the man.

Tom nearly toppled right into his lap, because he saw the square black boots planted wide apart on the paving almost too late.

'Sorry!' He poised, balancing over the flat cap. 'Didn't see you!'

'All right, all right. As long as you don't knock my bags over.'

There was a brown paper carrier by one foot, a big green bag by the other. They contained some kind of seed.

'Bird food?' Tom asked.

The man nodded.

'Two kinds? Whole bags full?'

The man was looking past him at the windblown, poke-necked pigeons, who always looked to Tom as if they owned the square, because there were nearly always more pigeons than people. Today the benches under the bare limes were empty.

'Do you give them whole *bags* full?' asked Tom again.

'I'm a bird fancier,' the man said.

He bent down and took a handful of corn from one of the carriers and tossed it out in

an expert curve of gold. The pigeons closed in, they all came and they were all drawn into a soft, grey-blue blot, like magic.

Tom stared, watching the eager nod of heads, hearing the soft patter of beaks on stone. It was as if he'd never seen pigeons before. Then slowly the blot spread, the feathers broke into separate birds again and you could see the stones in between. Tom sat down next to the bird fancier.

'Draughty,' his companion remarked.

Tom agreed. Draughty was right. After that they sat in silence, watching the pigeons make rings round the square. Tom took a sideways look. He could see only a thin slice of face between the upturned collar and downturned cap. Was he a tramp? Tom thought, he'd be in trouble if anyone saw the two of them together, side by side, as if they were old mates.

'Don't speak to strangers!'

'There's funny people about!'

He could hear his mother's voice and his teacher's, scolding in his head.

'It's broad daylight,' he told himself. 'And

we're sitting right in the middle of the square. Safe as houses.'

'Like birds, do you?' the old man asked.

'Sort of.'

Tom had never really thought about it. All he could say for certain was that on a grey Saturday in boring old Croxted, pigeons were one better than car numbers.

'Do it again,' he said, meaning throw the corn, and send the pigeons into a kaleidoscope.

'I bet they never make the same pattern twice,' he thought.

'Tom! Tommy!'

He winced. He knew the voice. Too right he did. And if she called him Tommy once more, he'd chuck stones and break every window in her house. (He wouldn't of course – for the very good reason that she lived right next door, and would have his guts for garters.)

'Tommy!'

He looked up and saw her – headscarf like a bandage round her long white face, eyes popping.

'Looks just as if someone had put a dish of rotten maggots right under her nose,' he thought. It was a look he knew well. He often came in for it.

'Tommy, what are you doing here?'

'Just sitting, Mrs Corner,' he told her. 'And my name's Tom.'

'And does your mother know?'

'Not exactly.'

How on earth did the daft bat think his mother could know he'd suddenly decided to sit down? Was she supposed to have a crystal ball, or something? He cringed at the thought of the lecture on the subject of dirty old tramps that was bound to follow.

'You didn't ought to be sitting here on your own,' she told him. 'You'd better come along with me, Tommy Briggs. D'you hear me?'

'Can't,' he told her. 'Collecting car numbers for a project, see.'

He fished out the notebook as proof.

'Then you do it somewhere else!'

He noted with interest that her white face, and her neck, were now a mottled pink. He must be bringing her out in a rash. He hoped it wasn't catching.

'I don't move from here until you do!'

Did she really think that the old man couldn't hear her? Tom looked sideways again, but could read nothing from the bird fancier's face.

It struck Tom that in a curious way he seemed not to be there. Of course he was there, but as if in another world. A glass wall seemed to separate him from the hissing Mrs Corner.

Mrs Corner now dumped both her shopping bags down beside the frayed carriers that held the bird fancier's seed.

'Here!' she snapped. 'You carry these!'

Tom stared up at her.

'You hear me?'

She turned and stomped off leaving the bags. He had no choice. She'd be straight round to his mother if he disobeyed. He sighed.

'Goodbye,' he said.

The bird fancier made no sign.

Mrs Corner had stopped, and was

waiting at the far side of the square. Seeing Tom with the bags, off she went again. For the thousandth time Tom wondered what on earth he had done to deserve having her as a next-door neighbour. He banged the bags hard against his legs as he went, and hoped they contained eggs, or cut glass.

Just then the sun came out. It came in a long sweeping band as if blown there by the wind. Tom turned and looked back.

The bird fancier and his bags were still there. Lit by the low winter sun they were gilded and sharp edged. And yet . . .

Tom stood and stared, aware that

something was odd, out of place. Maddeningly, he could not quite put his finger on what it was. The scene was like one of those pictures where you have to spot what is wrong — washing on the line blowing one way, for instance, and smoke from the chimney blowing another. Something like that. But what . . .?

Then he gasped. A chill that had nothing to do with the icy wind ran down his spine. He saw now what was out of kilter.

The bird fancier had no shadow.

He stared. He checked and checked again. It was true. The bird fancier — and his bags — were shadowless in that wide golden square.

And then the sun blew out again.

T W O

Tom caught up with Mrs Corner. He overtook her. He raced as if to keep up with his racing mind. The sooner he was home, the sooner he could turn about and run as fast as he had run in his life back to the shadowless figure in the square.

'Tommy!'

He heard his name blown after him and ignored it. It was not even as if it were his proper name.

He reached his house and waited for the buttoned-up figure just turning the corner of the street. He could hear the faint roaring of a crowd. His father had the football on, as usual. Tom peered through the front window and could see the screen on the far side of the room. Every single Saturday afternoon of his life those busy-looking men had run backwards and forwards over the green. Sometimes his father watched, sometimes he fell asleep. But come hell or high water the set stayed switched on.

'*That* was a nice race, I must say!'

Mrs Corner was out of breath.

'Give me those bags, and then you get inside. If only your mother knew – sat there alone, at your age!'

Tom was struck by a thought – an almost impossible thought. He hardly knew how to put it into words.

'Did you say *alone*?'

'Of course I did. You were, weren't you? I don't know. When I was your age, I – '

'But what about . . .?' He paused. He tried to choose his words carefully. 'What about the old man with the bags?'

She was staring at him now.

'The what with what?'

'You know – the old man sitting next to me.'

She shook her head.

'Give me those bags,' she said. He picked them up and passed them to her. His head buzzed. She had not seen the bird fancier!

He wondered if he were going mad. It could be the first sign – seeing people who weren't there, and talking to them. The next sign, he thought, could be seeing people with no shadows. There again, if they weren't there, how could they have shadows?

A picture rose again in his mind's eye of the long curve of thrown gold and the soft grey blot of pigeons. He had seen them, he was sure of it.

There was only one way to find out. He turned to retrace his steps. No sooner had he done so, than there was a sharp rap on the window. He turned. His father stood there, beckoning. Tom went back.

'So there you are! You get that car cleaned now!'

The words were muffled by the dividing glass. Tom groaned. He had clean forgotten.

'I'll do it later!' he shouted.

'It'll be dark. Get it done now, you hear me?'

Tom heard him. His father turned back to the busy screen.

'He'll have gone!' Tom thought. 'By the time I get back, he'll have gone!'

He believed this, but prayed for it not to be true. It seemed to him the most important thing in the world was that when he got back to the square, the bird fancier should still be there.

He ran through to the kitchen and fetched the bucket and sponge. The car was parked right in front of the house, and as Tom

sloshed and rubbed he could hear the cheering crowds, the roar as the ball thudded into the goal. It seemed impossible that the bird fancier should exist in the same world. Grimly Tom hung on to the thought of him, firmly planted in his craggy boots on the stone slabs of the square.

'He's real, he's real, he's real.' He chanted the words inside his head like a kind of charm.

The trouble was that underneath the chant lay the question, 'How can he be real, if he hasn't got a shadow?'

It wouldn't go away.

'And even if he is still there, how do I know he's real?'

The answer came, it came as effortlessly as magic.

'My camera!'

Tom had been given a camera for his last birthday. It was a Polaroid. For the first week he had photographed everything in sight. He couldn't get over the way the pictures developed, miraculously, almost as soon as you'd snapped them. It had seemed as if he was actually trapping time – turning it backwards, even.

Then the novelty had worn off. Now the camera lay on the drawers in his room, untouched for weeks.

'Perfect!' he told himself. 'The camera can't lie!'

That's what his father had said. It was true.

'If he's real, he'll come out on the photo!'

He didn't really want to think about what it would mean if the bird fancier didn't show up, if he ended up with a picture of the Market Square and an empty seat . . .

Tom sloshed a last bucketful of water over the car and took the cleaning things back. He poked his head round the living-room door.

'Done it, Dad!'

His father, eyes fixed on the screen, did not even look up.

'Good lad.'

Tom went up the stairs then, two at a time. It had suddenly occurred to him that there might not be a film in the camera.

'There is!'

Joyfully Tom raced down the stairs and out. He slammed the front door and ran.

He sped past the terraced houses, each with its glimpse of screen and muffled roar of crowds. The whole of Croxted, it seemed, was lost in a football match being played a hundred miles away. And all the time, at the very centre of the town, was a visitor from elsewhere. A visitor who conjured up real birds with real corn, yet had no shadow.

The bird fancier had to be there. Tom willed and wished him there, teeth gritted.

When he reached the square he halted, panting. Then he raised his eyes, hardly daring to look.

The bird fancier was there. He sat solid and immovable as if he were carved in stone. The wind and the pigeons rushed and tumbled about him.

Tom walked over. He kept his eyes fixed on the old man, half believing that he might melt into air.

'I'm back,' he said.

The wind was blowing the frayed flaps of the bird fancier's coat. 'Surely the wind can only blow what is actually there?' thought Tom.

'Ah. Well.'

Tom sat down. He was back just where he had been before.

'Have you run out of corn?'

For his answer the bird fancier leaned and took a fistful of grains from the brown carrier. With a single, expert flick the corn went curving into the wind and the pigeons went into storm again.

Tom watched the grey-blue blot form on the stone, then spread.

'It's very interesting,' he said. 'Watching them, I mean.'

This seemed a suitable remark to make to a bird fancier, but it got no reply. Tom tried again. What he wanted to know was, who the old man was, and where he came from. Was he a tramp? This seemed a rude question to ask outright.

'Er – do you come here often?' he asked.

There was a very long silence.

'I come when I'm bidden.'

Tom sat and chewed this over. 'Bidden' was a funny word. You didn't hear people say it, but he thought he might have come across it in books.

'Where you're asked, you mean?'

The frayed cap nodded, once.

'You mean you go *anywhere*?'

'World Traveller,' said the old man. 'I'm a World Traveller.'

Tom supposed this meant that he was a kind of Super Tramp. You had to be a Super *something* if you had no shadow. He very much wanted to ask about this, but didn't quite know how. Again, it seemed rude if you said straight out, 'Look, do you realise you haven't got a shadow?' It sounded like criticism.

Tom felt for the camera, in his jacket pocket. He wondered how he could actually produce it and take a photo, just like that?

The bird fancier got up.

'Are you going?' Tom was aghast.

'Time for the next pitch.'

Even as he spoke the clock of the town hall whirred and began to strike four. The dusk seemed to fall all in a moment, as if the clock had reminded it. The pigeons flew up and the bird fancier walked straight under the cloud they made.

He was going. He was going to leave Tom back where he'd found him, in a grey world of car numbers and identical flickering screens in a thousand darkening rooms. Tom jumped up and followed.

THREE

'Where is the next pitch?' asked Tom, catching up.

The bird fancier had said he was a World Traveller. If so, he could be going to the ends of the earth. And if so, Tom would try to follow.

'Park.'

Tom, who had not quite worked out where the ends of the earth were, and how he'd get there, was relieved.

'Can I come? I'll carry one of your bags if you like.'

The bird fancier passed over the brown carrier. They turned together up Market Street where the wind funnelled down in a long cold rush. It filled Tom's mouth and kept him speechless till they reached the park.

A few children were playing on the swings and slides at the far side in the fading light.

'This'll be the place,' said the bird fancier.

He sat on a bench under the rocking, leafless trees. Tom looked about. The stretch of grass before them was deserted. The trees were bare, the sky was packed with chimneys. He wondered why on earth he was there.

'Not many pigeons,' he remarked.

'Enough,' replied the bird fancier. 'If there weren't any, that would be awkward.'

'Awkward for what?'

'For what you might call my purposes.'

'Oh.'

They went on sitting. First the bird fancier had said hardly anything. Now that he was talking, he was talking in riddles. If it got really dark, and the moon came up and everything had a sharp black shadow except the bird fancier, Tom expected he would run away. There was a limit to how much mystery you could take, close to.

'I wish *I* was a World Traveller,' Tom heard himself say out of the blue. 'Freezing mucky old town.'

'Freezing, maybe. But mucky is as mucky does.'

'What's that supposed to mean?' demanded Tom. He didn't care whether he sounded rude or not. He felt rude. The cold was even making his fillings hurt.

'You mind your tone. If you want a proper answer to a question, you ask it proper, see?'

'Sorry.' Tom felt his cheeks grow hot.

'Own fault, I suppose. Go round looking like this and you can't expect manners.'

'You can!' Tom's face burned now. 'I don't care what you look like! Nor does anyone. What's it matter? And anyway,' he groped for the phrase and found it, ' – and anyway, fine feathers don't make fine birds!'

The effect of his words was electrifying.

'Oooooh!' roared the bird fancier. He bellowed. He slapped his thigh. His head went back and he snatched at his cap to save it.

'Oooh, don't they! Don't they just! Fancy anyone saying that to *ME!* Oh, it's rich, that is! It's rich!'

It seemed as if he would never get over it. The whole park rang with his laughter, but there was no one left to hear it now. They had all gone home. It was almost a waste of such marvellous mirth.

The laughter went on for so long that Tom found himself faintly miffed. It wasn't as if he shared the joke. He had no idea

what he could have said to provoke such prodigious laughter.

'So what's so funny?' he asked at last.

'You know something?' said the bird fancier slowly. 'I reckon I know why I'm here now.'

'What d'you mean? Don't you *know* what you're doing here?'

'I can do what I do anywhere. Up hill down dale, night and day, come wind come rain, moon –'

'All right,' said Tom. 'I get the picture.'

'What did you think when you saw me first?'

'Think?'

'When you saw me sitting there.'

'I don't know, exactly. And I didn't see

31

you, I bumped right into you, remember? I was treading on cracks in the paving and wishing – '

He broke off. He wasn't about to admit he'd been wishing for a few snarling bears, to liven things up.

'Ah!' The bird fancier sounded satisfied, as if he had the answer he wanted. 'Wishing . . .'

There was another long silence.

'You know something,' said the bird fancier, 'I've half a mind to show you something.'

'H – have you?'

'Half a mind – nay, I'm bound to! I shall! What's a joke if not to share? You watch!'

He took a handful of grain from the brown carrier. It went out in a clean swerve. The pigeons gathered, shaping out of the dusk.

'What about it?' Tom was blank.

The bird fancier looked at him again.

'You don't know me, and I don't know you,' he said. 'Right?'

'Right.'

'So there's no tales told, and no harm done. I'm here today but I'll be gone tomorrow. Now you wait. You watch this.'

He stooped down and took a handful of grain from the other bag this time, the green one. A curve of gold sped from hand to turf. The pigeons took no notice. It was amazing. They walked among the scattered grain as if it were invisible, not there at all.

Tom looked at the bird fancier, whose face was alive now and suddenly different, and then back at the turf.

'It's nearly all gone!' He simply could not believe his eyes. The pigeons had gone now. 'Where's it all gone?'

He strained into the gloom and the seeds were disappearing under his very eyes. They were like flakes of snow melting. Then, for a moment, he thought he heard a beating of wings, and scanned rapidly about him. The trees were empty, the sky blank.

'What's happening?' Tom cried. 'Something's happening, isn't it? I can't see. What is it?'

'You do it,' the bird fancier told him.

33

'Take a handful out of this green bag, and throw it. Just like I did.'

Tom hesitated – but only for a moment. He put his hand into the slithering seed and, grasping a fistful, flung it out as far as he could.

'Now!' said the bird fancier. 'Now do you see?'

But Tom did not answer. He did see, and what he saw was impossible, it had to be.

He saw birds, flocks of them. They were not pigeons or sparrows or starlings or blackbirds, or any other birds he had ever seen in his whole life before. They were beautiful, shining, blazing colour in the slow dusk.

'What's happening?' he heard his own voice cry. 'Where've they come from?'

'Out of the blue,' the bird fancier said.

'But they haven't!'

Tom's eyes fixed on a bird as blue and yellow as a gas jet. Then a red one, best of all, a red fire of feathers.

'You don't get birds like this in England!'

'Got some beauties, have you?' the bird fancier asked.

'Look – look at that one! What is it?'

The bird fancier shook his head.

'You tell me,' he said.

'That one – the green one with the curved beak!'

'Nay,' said the bird fancier.

'Can't you see it?'

'You don't see *my* birds,' the old man said, 'and I don't see yours. Private, see, these kinds of birds.'

'You mean you actually can't see them?'

'That's what I mean. If you want me to see them, you'll have to describe 'em to me. Or make a picture.'

A picture! Tom remembered the Polaroid then, still in his jacket pocket. Just as his fingers touched it, suddenly, terribly, the birds had gone. The dark was suddenly darker, as it is after a firework has exploded.

'They've gone! Where are they? Why've they gone?'

He did not wait for an answer. He plunged his hand into the bag again and hurled a frantic fistful of seed.

'Ah!'

There they were again, all of them, drawn by that magic seed.

Some had flown up to the boughs, and there he found his red one again, his favourite, plumage falling in a long blaze. Others wore crests, crowns. Some had legs as long as cranes' and snapping thin as glass. And they all walked and pecked and nodded in the windy park, as much at home

as the greedy town pigeons themselves.

The seeds had almost gone. This time Tom could almost see the bright feathers dwindle like sparks.

'More! More!' He reached for the bag. The bird fancier forestalled him.

'Time for the next pitch,' he said.

Tom groaned. The bird fancier was a World Traveller. The next pitch could be China or Timbuktu or the ends of the earth.

'Where?' he demanded. 'Where's the next pitch?'

'Station.'

Tom let out a yelp of delight.

'I live on Station Street! I'm coming with you!'

He reached for the green bag, but the bird fancier tucked it firmly under his arm and handed him the brown carrier instead.

'What seed *is* it?'

The old man had turned now and was plodding towards the high, wrought-iron gates.

'It's not corn, is it? Not ordinary seed? The pigeons didn't even see it!'

'That,' said the bird fancier, 'is exactly what you're finding out. You're only at the start of it yet. Wished, didn't you?'

'I – yes, in a way, sort of.'

'First step,' said the bird fancier. 'First step – wish. See how we go on from there, shall we?'

Tom did not reply. Things were just about as mysterious as he could stand them being, for now.

F O U R

Tom walked by the bird fancier's side and felt a stranger in his own town. He felt a stranger to himself, if it came to that.

'If I'd gone with Jake,' he thought, 'none of this would ever have happened.'

If he had gone with Jake on an ordinary bus to the ordinary fair, the world would have stayed ordinary. Time would have passed, as it always does, and by now he would be on an ordinary bus home. And the afternoon would be gone, finished, just another ordinary Saturday afternoon among all the others.

'Where do they come from?' he demanded suddenly, and a thousand other questions came crowding after.

'They're *my* birds,' the bird fancier said.

'But they're not! *I* saw them, as well!'

'Maybe you did, maybe you didn't.'

'I did!'

Tom had seen birds that had never before visited a wintry park. He had seen jungle birds on bare boughs. He was not even sure that such birds existed even in jungles.

They went back down to the square without another word. Tom saw the lighted buses going by and the pale faces turned to the windows, and wondered if they knew that the town was full of invisible birds.

In the square the bird fancier stopped.

'Get my breath,' he said, and sat heavily on the bench where Tom had first found him.

Tom thrust his hands in his pockets for warmth and jogged gently on the spot. He was impatient for the last pitch, hoping for a miracle of some sort.

'Tom! Hey – Tom!'

It was Jake. Instinctively Tom moved away from the bench. He sensed some kind of threat to his shadowless visitor. Mrs

Corner had not even seen him. But Jake might – and break the spell.

'Birdspell!' The word came into Tom's head, newly minted. 'Birdspell.'

'Hey – you ought to've come! It was great!'

Tom looked at him.

'Where's my candy floss?' he asked.

'Sorry – ran out of money. Had two goes on that Dice with Death – phew! Honestly, it's the best yet! And look!'

He held out a plastic bag full of water. In it was a pale goldfish, flicking and turning.

'Won it! Won it first time!'

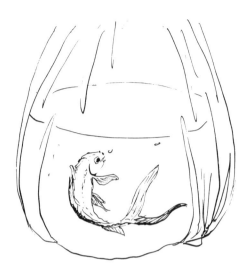

If he had, it would be a record, Tom thought. He'd been at fairs with Jake when he'd spent nearly two pounds to win a goldfish.

'Great,' he said.

'C'mon. If we're quick we'll see the end!'

'End of what?'

'The match, idiot. On the telly. Come on!'

'Can't.'

'Why not?'

Tom produced his notebook. Jake stared disbelievingly.

'You're barmy! You've never been all afternoon collecting that lot, and still – '

'I shan't be long,' Tom said. 'You go on and I'll catch you up.'

Jake was not listening. He was seeing straight through Tom just as Tom had seen through him.

'You're up to something,' he said. 'What?'

'Nothing.'

'Go on, tell.'

Tom actually found himself smiling at the idea of his telling Jake about the seed in the green bag.

Might as well tell him I've been to the moon and back, he thought.

'What're you grinning at?'

'I'm not.'

As he spoke, Tom saw the bird fancier. He had got his breath back and was now on his way again. And he was taking the route he and Jake would take, to get home. He was going to walk straight out of Tom's life and would never be seen again. He was going to dissolve like a dream.

'Oh clear off!' he said angrily. Jake was his best friend, but at that particular moment Tom did not care if he became his worst enemy.

'Have you gone mad, or something?'

'Just clear off!'

To his absolute amazement, Jake did just that. No argument – nothing. He just turned and went – ran, as if to catch up with the steadily plodding bird fancier.

Tom watched as the distance narrowed between the two figures. It began to look as if there would be a collision – or worse. It surely could not happen? His best friend could surely not run straight through the man without a shadow? Or could he . . .?

Tom chickened out. At the last minute he shut his eyes. When he opened them he caught a last glimpse of Jake flying up the parade – and the bird fancier was still there.

'Hurray!' Now Tom ran, too.

'Sorry – about that!' he gasped out the words as he caught up and fell into step. 'Friend of mine.'

The bird fancier did not reply. Perhaps Jake had been invisible to him, just as he

himself had been to Mrs Corner. Tom did not know or care.

They turned into Station Street. Tom could actually see his own house, down there at the far end, beyond the wide gate of the station itself. And inside it the screen was still flickering, his father dozing, his mother getting tea. It was impossible, all of it.

They reached the draughty station yard. The booking hall was deserted. Trains hardly ever stopped here any more. They just passed through. Pigeons huddled on the high girders and the sky showed through the broken glass of the roof. It was a ghost station.

'Last pitch,' said the bird fancier and sat down, sighing. 'I shall have to be getting along, soon.'

Tom's heart stopped. 'No! Don't go!'

The bird fancier had opened a window and now was going to bang it shut again, perhaps for ever. Tom reached for the green bag.

'Steady now,' warned the bird fancier. 'First things first. We don't want people looking.'

There was no one to look, but the corn from the brown bag was scattered all the same, and the pigeons came down. The sound of their beaks pattered like rain.

'Now!' cried Tom when the corn had gone. 'Let me!'

He plunged his hand into the green bag. He threw out the seed, handful after handful, because this was the last time and then the birds would melt into the dark for ever. Handful after handful he threw and hardly even felt the bird fancier tugging the bag from his grasp.

The great vault of the station filled with

colour, it blossomed under his eyes. Red, blue, green, yellow, violet – the colours glowed in the gloom. These birds were visitors from another place. Their plumage swept the cold stone and their eyes glittered.

'I shall have to be getting along,' the bird fancier said again, but Tom did not hear.

'I must get a picture,' he was thinking. 'That one, there, the one with the yellow comb . . .'

He took out the camera and raised it. Click!

The birds vanished. Tom blinked. Automatically he pulled out the film and placed it under his arm.

'Only a few seconds,' he told himself. 'Then I'll know.'

The bird fancier was looking at him strangely.

'That's not the way,' he said.

'Why? Why isn't it?'

'I told you. Your birds are in your head, mine are in mine.'

'Not *real*, you mean.'

'I mean,' said the bird fancier, 'that if you want other people to see them, you've got to *make* 'em real.'

Tom stared. Slowly, very slowly, he took out the photo and looked at it. There was the blank paving, the empty hall.

'Not there!'

'I told you.'

Desperately Tom ran and plunged his hand again into the green bag. They were there again, miraculous in that dingy place.

'What if I could *catch* one,' Tom thought. 'That one, there, with the red tail . . .'

He had got to his feet and began to move stealthily forward. As he approached the birds he realised that they were taking no notice of him. They behaved exactly as if he was not there. And so he walked straight among them towards the one he wanted, the one whose tail was a long scarlet thread of flame. His heart thudded. He felt like a thief, or a murderer.

'It's not as if I'm going to kill it,' he thought. 'I just want to catch it, and keep it.'

He was taking off his anorak as he went. It was so easy that at the very last minute he could hardly bring himself to do it. He spread the coat above the shining back and held it poised, like a black cloud.

'I *must* have it!' he thought fiercely, and dropped the anorak.

Afterwards Tom could never be quite certain, but he thought he had heard a screech, a loud sharp cry of protest. But all he really knew for certain was that in an instant the birds had gone. Tom snatched up his anorak – there was nothing under it.

'That's not the way,' he heard the bird fancier say.

'What *is* then?' Tom was desperate.

'I can't make your birds real because I don't even see them,' the bird fancier told him. 'Only you can do that.'

He moved slowly towards a heap of stone rubble, and eyed it.

'What I could do,' he said, 'though it's against all the rules, mind, is give you one of mine.'

'One of your birds?'

The bird fancier did not hear him.

'Why not . . . why not . . .?' he murmured to himself.

He stooped down and threw out a handful of seed from the green bag. Tom strained into the dimness and saw that the seed was disappearing, as it had before, melting like snow. The station was thronged with invisible birds.

'I *still* can't see them!' he cried. 'Please, please!'

Now the seeds had vanished, too. Tom turned.

'I thought you said – '

The bird fancier had gone. Tom stared. And yet – there was a movement from the heap of stone. It was as if it were alive – heaving, flowing, remaking itself. It was impossible.

The bird fancier's voice rang out, echoing vastly in that deserted hall.

'I'll show you the secret! Just this once. Now!'

Slowly, awestruck, Tom moved forward, his eyes fixed on the stone. And in the twinkling of an eye it was still again, and it had changed.

'*Now* do you see?' The bird fancier's triumphant voice filled the empty corners. 'That's the way!'

Tom shivered. It was amazing, miraculous. Fanfares of trumpets should be sounding, the sky opening. There should be thunder and lightning and a mighty wind. Something new had come into the world.

'I see it!' Tom yelled, and hurled his

anorak high into the air. 'I see it!'

* * *

Everyone knows now about the bird of paradise in Croxted Station. Everyone knows how it appeared suddenly, out of the blue, from one day to the next. No one can even guess how it came to be there. And the one person who knows does not tell.

When they found it they tried to move it, to put it in a gallery. But its stone feet were rooted to the stone platform. Curious sightseers wander in to see it from time to time, and wonder at how feathers can seem so soft in stone.

Tom goes in every day to see it. Only he knows that this is no statue, but real, and he can see a real bird under the grey stone. He touches gently the cold, tilted head. He strokes the smooth, curved beak. Sometimes he talks to the bird.

'Before, you were just a picture in someone's head,' he tells him. 'Now the whole world can see you. You're famous.'

The bird, of course, cannot reply. Nor can he see the paintings that line the wall of

Tom's room. There, he might recognise those other birds who had come with him flocking out of the darkness. Tom has learned the secret of how to make the birds in his head real.

He has made even the bird fancier real, head thrown back, craggy boots firmly planted.

'Who's that?' Tom's mother had asked.

'Oh, just someone I met.'

'You're getting to be a good little painter, Tom. What beautiful birds! What are they?'

'Oh, they just came out of thin air.'

This is truer than she knows. This is all she will ever know.

Tom has another secret, too. Later, he found a few seeds clinging to his anorak, and has planted them in a window box outside his room. Every day he waters them and at last, now spring is coming, tiny shoots of green are showing through.

Tom counts the days until the autumn, and his own small harvest. Because then he will know for certain whether or not the seed is the *right* seed.

And if it is, he'll have his own magic, and a skyful of his own birds, for ever.

FLOW
by Pippa Goodhart

'Please, Dad, Mum, please, please, can I have a dog?'
'Do you really think that you are responsible enough to look after a dog when you can't even look after yourself? The answer is a very definite "No"!'

But Oliver won't take no for an answer. Secretly he chooses Flow, the runt of the litter, who's a bit odd, a bit backward, but definitely the dog Oliver needs. Their first summer together takes an unexpected turn that will test them both to the limit.

In her first novel, runner-up for the Kathleen Fidler award, Pippa Goodhart interweaves an exciting adventure story with a warm sympathy with her hero's dyslexia. She shows that life throws up challenges that demand more than one kind of courage.

YOU CAN'T EAT YOUR CHICKEN POX, AMBER BROWN
by Paula Danziger

Amber Brown is in a bit of a spot.

Actually, she's covered with spots.

What's a kid to do?

It's her first trip to England.

And Amber gets Chicken Pox.

Will she ever be ready for London?

Will London ever be ready for Amber Brown?

THE PECKTHORN MONSTER
by Hazel Townson

'There's a monster in Peckthorn Woods!'

Suddenly the peaceful life of the whole village is threatened. No one knows what to do . . . except young Peter and his sister, Katy. Ignoring adult warnings, the children set off for the woods in search of the monster. But they are in for a great many shocks and surprises.

A delightfully zany comedy by a master storyteller, perfectly complemented by Philippe Dupasquier's witty illustrations.

SWAPPER
by Robert Leeson

It was no good going back and saying — I've changed my mind. No swap backs was Swapper's rule. Swapper was for real.

Scott secretly believes he can beat Swapper and so he begins a massive rolling swap, trading up day after day, so he can finally match Swapper and get a Rocket Island. He takes risks — anything goes, including his friendship with Davie. But in the end, Scott finds some things are for keeps, too good to swap.

Robert Leeson is the author of the popular *Zarnia* series. He received the Eleanor Farjeon Award for services to children and literature.

NANI'S HOLIDAY
by Lisa Bruce

'Why Jazeera, you're crying,' Nani said. 'What's wrong?'
Jazeera sniffed, then gulped.
'I'm . . . I'm happy. I'm so glad you're here, Nani.'
'So am I,' Nani whispered.
Nani put her arm around Jazeera and held her very tight.

When Nani comes to England from India for Salma's wedding, Jazeera has a chance to share her new life with her beloved grandmother.

It is Nani who helps her make a really big decision. It is Nani who links Jazeera's school with Anil, a penniless boy in India. It is Nani who teaches her the value of friendship.

But it is Jazeera who gives Nani the holiday of a lifetime . . .

This sequel to *Jazeera's Journey* is a satisfying family story that bridges two worlds. *Jazeera's Journey* was described as a 'sensitive, multicultural story . . . Touching and evocative' in the *Gloucestershire Echo*.

JOHN MIDAS AND THE VAMPIRES
by Patrick Skene Catling

A giant bat with wings as black as midnight suddenly flapped horribly squealing from the highest turret of the castle . . . Now the bat's red eyes were close . . . John Midas knew that in a moment he would be eaten. As he expected, everything went black, except for the dreadful words: "GAME OVER."

John has lost this video game, but practice makes perfect — so much so that he becomes Junior Pretendo Champion of Britain and wins a family holiday to Gothic World in Transylvania, once home of Count Dracula.

Despite the emphasis on red and a rather unusual swimming pool, Gothic world seems a trifle ordinary. But then John and his sister Mary buy a model vampire bat that can really fly . . . Now the real horror begins.

A wonderfully flesh-creeping adventure of the hero of *The Chocolate Touch* and *John Midas and the Radio Touch*.